Winnie-the-Pooh
A Party
For Pooh

Adapted from the stories by A. A. Milne

One day, when the sun had come back over the Forest, all the streams of the Forest were tinkling happily to find themselves their own pretty shape again. The little pools lay dreaming of the life they had seen and the big things they had done. In the warmth and quiet of the Forest, wood-pigeons were complaining gently to themselves in their lazy, comfortable way that it was the other fellow's fault, but it didn't matter very much. On such a day as this, Christopher Robin whistled in a special way he had, and Owl came flying out of the Hundred Acre Wood to see what was wanted.

"Owl," said Christopher Robin, "I am going to give a party."

"You are, are you?" said Owl.

"And it's to be a special sort of party, because it's because of what Pooh did when he did what he did to save Piglet from the flood."

"Oh, that's what it's for, is it?" said Owl, helpfully.

"Yes, so will you tell Pooh as quickly as you can and all the others too, because it will be tomorrow?"

"Oh, it will, will it?" said Owl, still being as helpful as possible.

"So will you go and tell them, Owl?" said Christopher Robin.

Owl tried to think of something wise to say, but he couldn't, so he flew off to tell the others. The first person he told was Pooh.

"Pooh," he said. "Christopher Robin is giving a party."

"Oh!" said Pooh. And then seeing that Owl expected him to say something else, he said, "Will there be those little cake things with pink sugar icing?"

Owl felt that it was rather beneath him to talk about little cake things with pink sugar icing, so he told Pooh exactly what Christopher Robin had said, and then flew off to Eeyore.

"A party for Me?" thought Pooh to himself. "How grand!" And he began to wonder if all the other animals would know that it was a special Pooh Party, and if Christopher Robin had told them about *The Floating Bear* and the *Brain of Pooh* and all the wonderful ships he had invented and sailed on.

While Pooh was thinking about this, Owl was talking to Eeyore.

"Eeyore," said Owl, "Christopher Robin is giving a party."

"That's very interesting," said Eeyore. "I suppose they will be sending me down the odd bits of food which got trodden on. Very Kind and Thoughtful. Not at all, don't mention it."

"There is an Invitation for you, too," said Owl.

"What's that like?"

"An Invitation!" said Owl.

"Yes, I heard you. Who dropped it?" asked Eeyore.

"It isn't something to eat, it's asking you to the party tomorrow!"

Eeyore shook his head slowly.

"I think you mean Piglet," he said. "The little fellow with the excited ears. That's Piglet, I'll tell him."

"No, no," said Owl, getting quite fussy. "It's you!"

"Are you sure?" said Eeyore.

"Of course I'm sure! Christopher Robin said 'All of them! Tell all of them,'" said Owl.

"All of them, except Eeyore?" asked Eeyore.

"*All* of them," said Owl, sulkily.

"Ah!" said Eeyore. "A mistake, no doubt, but still, I shall come. Only don't blame *me* if it rains."

But it didn't rain. Christopher Robin had made a long table out of some long pieces of wood, and they all sat round it. Christopher Robin sat at one end, and Pooh sat at the other, and between them on one side were Owl and Eeyore and Piglet, and between them on the other side were Rabbit, and Roo and Kanga. It was the first party to which Roo had ever been, and he was very excited. As soon as they had all sat down, he began to talk.

"Hallo, Pooh!" he squeaked.

"Hallo, Roo!" said Pooh.

Roo jumped up and down in his seat for a little while and then began again.

"Hallo, Piglet!" he squeaked.

Piglet waved a paw at him, being too busy to say anything.

"Hallo, Eeyore!" said Roo.

Eeyore nodded gloomily at him. "It will rain soon, you see if it doesn't," he said.

Roo looked up to see if it didn't, and it didn't, so he said "Hallo, Owl," and Owl said, "Hallo, my little fellow," in a kindly way, and went on talking to Christopher Robin.

Kanga said to Roo, "Drink up your milk first, dear, and talk afterwards." So Roo, who was drinking his milk, tried to say that he could do both at once . . . and had to be patted on the back and dried for quite a long time afterwards.

When they had all nearly eaten enough,
Christopher Robin banged on the table with
his spoon and everybody stopped talking and
was very silent.

"This party," said Christopher Robin, "is a party because of what someone did. We all know who it was, and it's his party because of what he did, and I've got a present for him and here it is." Then he felt about a little and whispered, "Where is it?"

While Christopher Robin was looking, Eeyore coughed in an impressive way and began to speak.

"Friends," he said. "It is a great pleasure, or perhaps I had better say it has been a pleasure so far, to see you at my party. What I did was nothing. Any of you – except Rabbit and Owl and Kanga – would have done the same. Oh, and Pooh. My remarks do not of course, apply to Piglet and Roo, because they are too small. Any of you would have done the same. But it just happened to be Me. It was not, I need hardly say, with an idea of getting what Christopher Robin is looking for now." He put his front leg to his mouth and said in a loud whisper, "Try under the table" – "that I did what I did, because I feel we should all do what we can to help. I feel that we should all –"

"What's Eeyore talking about?" Piglet whispered to Pooh.

"I don't know," said Pooh rather dolefully.

"I thought this was *your* party," said Piglet.

"I thought it was *once*. But I suppose it isn't."

"I'd sooner it was yours than Eeyore's," said Piglet.

"So would I," said Pooh.

"AS – I – WAS – SAYING," said Eeyore, rather loudly and sternly, "as I was saying when I was interrupted by various Loud Sounds, I feel that –"

"Here it is!" cried Christopher Robin excitedly. "Pass it down to silly old Pooh. It's for Pooh."

"For Pooh?" said Eeyore.

"Of course it is. He's the best bear in all the world!" said Christopher Robin.

"I might have known," said Eeyore. "After all, one can't complain. I have my friends. Somebody spoke to me only yesterday."

Nobody was listening to Eeyore, for they were all saying, "Open it, Pooh." And of course, Pooh was opening it as quickly as ever he could, without cutting the string, because you never know when a bit of string might be Useful. And at last, it was undone.

When Pooh saw what it was, he nearly fell down, he was so pleased. It was a Special Pencil Case. There were pencils in it marked 'B' for Bear, and 'HB' for Helping Bear and 'BB' for Brave Bear.

There was a little knife for sharpening the pencils, and a rubber for rubbing out anything which you had spelt wrong. There was a ruler for ruling lines for the words to walk on and inches marked on the ruler in case you wanted to know how many inches anything was. There were Blue Pencils and Red Pencils and Green Pencils for saying special things in blue and red and green. And all these lovely things were in little pockets of their own in the Special Case which shut with a click when you clicked it. And they were all for Pooh!

"Oh!" said Pooh.

"Oh, Pooh!" said everybody else, except Eeyore.

"Thank you," growled Pooh.

Later on, when they had all said "Goodbye" and "Thank you" to Christopher Robin, Pooh and Piglet walked home thoughtfully together in the golden evening. For a long time they were silent.

"When you wake up in the morning, Pooh," said Piglet at last, "what's the first thing you say to yourself?"

"What's for breakfast?" said Pooh. "What do *you* say, Piglet?"

"I say, I wonder what exciting things are going to happen?" said Piglet.

Pooh nodded thoughtfully.

"It's the same thing," he said.

This edition published in Great Britain 2002
First published in 2000 by Egmont Books Limited
239 Kensington High Street, London W8 6SA
Copyright © 2002 Michael John Brown, Peter Janson-Smith,
Roger Hugh Vaughan Charles Morgan and Timothy Michael
Robinson, Trustees of the Pooh Properties.
Published under licence from The Walt Disney Company.
Adapted from *Winnie-the-Pooh*, first published 1926.
Text by A.A. Milne and line drawings by E.H. Shepard
copyright under the Berne Convention.
New and adapted line drawings and colouring of the illustrations
by Stuart Trotter copyright © 2000 Egmont Books Limited
All Rights Reserved.
ISBN 1 4052 0157 6
1 3 5 7 9 10 8 6 4 2
Printed in China.